Stories for Boys

Featuring Sinbad and the Giant, Pinocchio and Aladdin

igloo

Sinbad and the Giant

Once upon a time, there was a fearless sailor named Sinbad. Sinbad and his brave crew sailed the seven seas, exploring strange, new lands and looking for rare and exotic goods to trade. Often, their searches led them into dangerous adventures, but none was as deadly as Sinbad's encounter with the one-eyed giant.

Sinbad was sailing back to his home, with a ship laden with treasure, when a mighty storm blew up. Huge waves rose higher than the mast and crashed down on the deck. Thunder rattled above the ship and lightning blasted down to strike the mast. Sinbad and his men were thrown into the sea.

When the storm cleared, the sailors found themselves washed up on a deserted island. There was no sign of their ship. The crew explored the island, but the only animals they could find were a herd of sheep grazing on a grassy hill. As Sinbad climbed the hill, he saw a mighty fortress on the other side. Its great doors were open, so Sinbad and his men stumbled inside. There they found an empty courtyard. It was lined with tall doors, all of which were closed. Sinbad and his men were exhausted. They soon fell asleep in the courtyard.

The sailors woke up to a thundering sound so loud, they thought the storm had returned. But it was not the storm. A flock of sheep had run into the courtyard. They were followed by a mighty giant. It was his footsteps that were making so much noise. The giant was as tall as four men standing on each others' shoulders. He was fierce and foul-smelling and he had a single eye in the middle of his forehead.

The men tried to escape, but the giant had closed the great doors behind them. "What's this?" roared the giant. "I can smell human beings!" The giant peered at them with his huge eye. Sinbad noticed that the giant couldn't see very well. However, the giant managed to grab Sinbad. "You're very skinny," said the giant, throwing Sinbad to the ground. He picked up another man and felt him all over. "Another skinny one," he said, grumpily, throwing the sailor down.

The ship's cook was a much fatter man. He tried to run from the giant, but the giant scooped him up easily. "That's more like it," bellowed the giant. "Tomorrow night, I will make a big fire and roast you for my dinner!" The giant opened one of the big doors and went into his castle, leaving Sinbad and his men trapped in the gloomy courtyard.

The poor cook was terrified that he was going to be eaten. "Don't worry," said Sinbad. "When the giant lets his sheep out tomorrow morning, we'll rush out, too." So, the next morning, when the giant opened his gates to let the sheep out, Sinbad and his men tried to leave. But the giant saw them and slammed the heavy gate shut before they could get out.

That night, when the giant came back in, he made a fire and tried to find the cook. But Sinbad was too clever for the giant. He hid the fat cook in a pile of sheepskins that were lying in a corner of the courtyard. Then he marched up to the giant. "Look what you've done to me," said Sinbad, trying to sound like the cook. "I'm so frightened, I've become nothing more than skin and bone."

The giant picked Sinbad up. "You're not worth eating," he said. He threw Sinbad and his men some mutton, which they ate, hungrily. "I'll fatten you up, then eat you tomorrow night," said the giant, going to bed inside his castle.

"How will we get out?" asked the fat cook, coming out from under the sheepskins. Sinbad looked at the sheepskins. "I think I have a plan," he said.

The next morning, when the giant went to let his sheep out, he found that Sinbad and his crew had built a big, smoky fire. The giant could hardly see anything. "You're not getting out," he yelled. As he let his sheep out, he felt along each one's back, to make sure it wasn't Sinbad, or his men. "That's funny," said the giant. "I have more sheep than I thought."

The giant didn't realise that Sinbad and his crew had put sheepskins over their backs and walked out on all fours, pretending to be sheep.

Sinbad and his men ran to the other side of the island and chopped down some trees to make big rafts. By evening, they were almost ready to sail.

However, when the giant herded his sheep back to his castle that night, he realised that the men were gone. "I've been tricked!" he boomed and Sinbad could hear it from the other side of the island.

The giant stomped all over the island, looking all around with his one, giant eye. As Sinbad tied the last of the logs to the raft, he made sure everyone was on it. "Set sail!" he cried and the men raised the sheepskin sails.

Just as they were pushing off the raft, the giant saw them. He waded right into the sea. The sailors paddled as fast as they could, but the wind kept blowing them backwards. The giant was up to his neck in the ocean, but he raised his huge hands and tried to smash the raft.

"Cut down the mast," cried Sinbad. The sailors were amazed, but they did what they were told. The tall mast of the raft toppled over and struck the angry giant on the head. The giant sunk right to the bottom of the ocean and never troubled anybody again.

"Now we are stuck in the sea without a mast, we'll never get home," said the fat cook, sadly.
"There's something on the horizon," said one of the men. "It's our ship!"

Sure enough, Sinbad's ship had survived the storm. Sinbad and his men sailed back home with all their treasure and a wonderful story of a one-eyed giant to tell.

Pinocchio

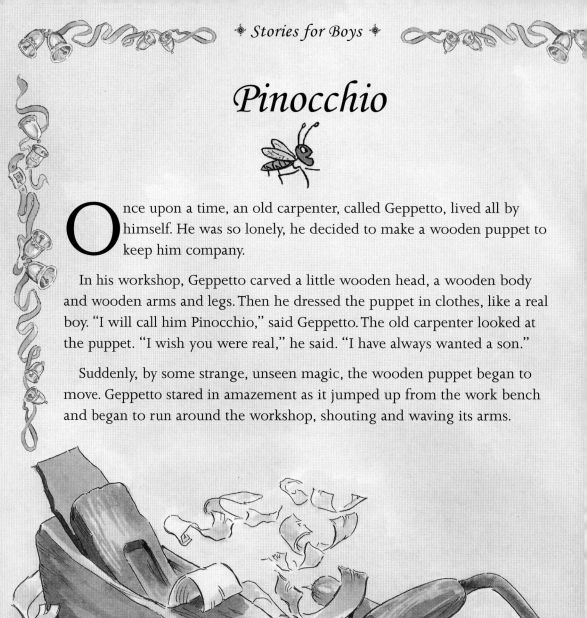

Once upon a time, an old carpenter, called Geppetto, lived all by himself. He was so lonely, he decided to make a wooden puppet to keep him company.

In his workshop, Geppetto carved a little wooden head, a wooden body and wooden arms and legs. Then he dressed the puppet in clothes, like a real boy. "I will call him Pinocchio," said Geppetto. The old carpenter looked at the puppet. "I wish you were real," he said. "I have always wanted a son."

Suddenly, by some strange, unseen magic, the wooden puppet began to move. Geppetto stared in amazement as it jumped up from the work bench and began to run around the workshop, shouting and waving its arms.

Pinocchio

Geppetto was overjoyed. He did not understand why his wooden puppet had come to life, but he was very happy. "Pinocchio," said Geppetto, "I am your father and tomorrow you will go to school. Maybe, one day, if you learn enough, you will become a real boy."

That night, when Pinocchio went to bed, he dreamed that a beautiful fairy visited him. "I am the Blue Fairy who looks after all boys – real, or wooden," she said. "I have brought you a friend to help you to be good." The Blue Fairy waved her wand and a tiny cricket appeared.

The cricket was able to speak. "Hello, Pinocchio," it said. "I will be your friend and help you to behave properly, like a real boy. Tomorrow, we shall go to school together."

The next morning, Pinocchio went downstairs with the cricket. Geppetto was very proud that his little wooden son was going to school. "Here are five gold coins to buy school books with," he said. "It's all the money I have in the world, so spend it wisely."

"Yes, Father," said Pinocchio. But the wooden puppet was lying. He did not want to go to school, or spend the money on school books. Suddenly, Pinocchio's wooden nose grew longer. Geppetto looked at it and frowned. "Pinocchio," he said, "why is your nose growing?" But the puppet just grabbed the gold coins, shoved them into his pocket and ran out of the door.

The clever cricket knew that the puppet's nose had changed because he had told a lie. From that moment on, each time Pinocchio lied, his nose grew longer.

Meanwhile, outside the house, Pinocchio heard lovely music. "Let's go to school," said the cricket, but Pinocchio ignored him and followed the music, which led to a travelling puppet theater.

"I am going to stay here and become a performer," said Pinocchio. "My father won't mind." But when he said this, Pinocchio's nose grew, which meant he was lying.

The cricket tried to stop Pinocchio, but the puppet would not listen. Instead of going to school, he travelled with the theater to a distant land, near the sea.

Poor Geppetto looked everywhere for his precious, wooden son. But Pinocchio was nowhere to be found.

After many days, the cricket persuaded Pinocchio to go back home. They set off and Pinocchio jangled Geppetto's five, gold coins in his pockets, as he walked.

Nearby, a cunning cat and a sly fox heard the money jangling. "Where are you going, little wooden boy?" they asked. Pinocchio told them that he was going home to see his father. "Your father will make you go to school, when you could be having fun in the Land of Play," said the sly fox.

"However," said the cat. Nobody who has any money can get in. Money isn't allowed in the Land of Play."

Pinocchio gave the fox and the cat all of his money. He would not listen to the cricket who told him not to. "Tell me the way to the Land of Play," begged Pinocchio, "I want to go there now."

The cat and the fox told Pinocchio where to go. Then they ran off, laughing at how they had tricked the silly puppet out of his money.

"Please, Pinocchio, go home to your father," pleaded the cricket. "I don't want to see my father," snapped the puppet. Suddenly, his nose grew longer. Pinocchio secretly missed Geppetto, but he refused to go home.

The Land of Play was a huge fair. There were sweets and rides and lots of games to play. It was filled with children who didn't want to go to school and Pinocchio spent many weeks there.

Meanwhile, Geppetto was sick with worry. He searched all over the land for Pinocchio, but there was no sign of him anywhere. Finally, Geppetto reached the sea. "Pinocchio must have crossed the water," he thought. Geppetto built a raft to look for his son. However, far out on the ocean, the raft was swallowed by a huge shark and Geppetto found himself in its belly.

In the Land of Play, Pinocchio didn't notice the days passing until his ears began to feel strange. They were long and floppy, like donkey's ears. Then, when he looked behind him, Pinocchio noticed that he had grown a donkey's tail.

"All children who stay here turn into donkeys," said the cricket. "We must escape, before you become one, too, Pinocchio."

However, the gates of the Land of Play were shut. The only way out was by sea, so Pinocchio and the cricket jumped into the water.

Great waves rolled and the wild sea tossed the pair up and down. After many hours, a huge shark swam by and swallowed the exhausted friends.

It was dark inside the shark's belly. Suddenly, Pinocchio heard a voice – it was Geppetto! "I'm sorry that I lied and ran away, Father," sobbed Pinocchio.

Geppetto hugged his wooden son. "I forgive you," he said. They all danced for joy and the movement gave the shark such a belly-ache, it spat them out and they were washed up on the shore.

After that, Pinocchio promised to be good and this time, his nose didn't grow. Instead, the Blue Fairy appeared. "Pinocchio, you have learned to tell the truth," she said. "Now you are a real boy."

Pinocchio felt the donkey ears and tail disappear. Suddenly, his wooden body was soft and warm. He was a real boy! Pinocchio, Geppetto and the cricket returned home and lived in peace and happiness ever after.

Aladdin

Long ago, in a great city, there lived a poor, hungry orphan boy named Aladdin. He had no home of his own, so he had to live on the streets and steal food to survive.

One day, a wealthy-looking man called to Aladdin in the marketplace. Aladdin thought the man was about to punish him for stealing and he tried to hide. "Don't be afraid," said the man. "I am your long-lost uncle, Abenazer. If you will help me, Aladdin, together we will make our fortune."

Aladdin didn't know that Abenazer was not really his uncle, but a wicked magician. Abenazer wanted a magic lamp that lay in an enchanted cave nearby, but he was cowardly and wanted Aladdin to get it for him.

Abenazer took Aladdin to the cave entrance, which was a small hole that led down a steep slope. "You may take all the treasure you find inside," said Abenazer. "Just bring me the dirty old lamp from the middle of the cave."

Aladdin went into the cave. He had never seen so much treasure. Gold was piled in heaps on the floor and the walls of the cave were covered with precious stones. Aladdin filled his pockets with jewels. He found a gold ring on the floor and put it on his finger.

Aladdin found the old lamp on a large stone in the middle of the cave. He took the lamp, but the moment it was in his hands, the floor started to shake. Aladdin looked up to find the entrance to the cave closing above him. Climbing as fast as he could, he reached the opening of the cave. "Help me out, Uncle," cried Aladdin.

"Give me the lamp first," said Abenazer. He tried to grab the lamp, but he knocked Aladdin, who was still holding it, down the rocky slope. Aladdin tumbled back down into the cave and when he looked up, the entrance to the cave had closed behind him.

Aladdin sat in the dark, wondering what to do. He was trapped in the cave. "That man was no uncle of mine," he said, rubbing the dirty lamp to clean it. "How I wish I had some light in here."

Suddenly, a mighty, green genie whooshed from the spout of the lamp. The genie made more lamps appear, so the cave was flooded with light.

"I am the genie of the lamp. My wish is your command. What is your next wish, Master?" said the genie.

Aladdin was amazed. "I wish I were at home," he said. The genie clicked his fingers and Aladdin was back in the marketplace, surrounded by the jewels he was carrying.

From then on, the genie appeared every time Aladdin rubbed the lamp. It could make all of Aladdin's wishes come true. "I wish for a great palace!" cried Aladdin. The ground shook and a mighty, marble palace rose from the desert. It was bigger than the palace of the sultan himself.

Soon, Aladdin was the richest man in the city. He married the sultan's daughter and they lived happily in their desert palace.

However, Abenazer had not forgotten Aladdin. When he found out that Aladdin had the lamp, he came up with a plan to get the lamp and use its power for himself.

Abenazer disguised himself as a poor lamp-seller. Then, he went to Aladdin's palace with a cart full of new lamps, "New lamps for old!" he cried.

Aladdin's wife didn't know that Aladdin's lamp was magical. She gave Abenazer the old magic lamp, in return for a shiny new one.

As soon as Abenazer had the lamp, he told the genie to take away all Aladdin's wealth and his palace. Abenazer made himself sultan and imprisoned Aladdin's wife. Aladdin was a poor man, once again.

All that Aladdin had left was the gold ring he had taken from the enchanted cave. "I must sell it to buy food," Aladdin thought. "But I don't know how I can get my wife and my palace back."

Aladdin cleaned the ring with an old rag and suddenly, a great, blue genie whooshed out of it. "I am the genie of the ring," said the genie. "What is your wish?"

Aladdin asked the genie of the ring to restore his power, but the genie could not. "The genie of the lamp is more powerful than me," explained the genie of the ring. "I cannot reverse his magic."

Aladdin asked the genie to take him to Abenazer. In the blink of an eye, he was outside the sultan's palace. Through the windows, he could see that Abenazer had become Sultan.

Aladdin thought of a cunning plan to get his lamp back. "Genie of the ring," he said. "I wish for a potion that will send anyone who drinks it to sleep."
"Your wish is my command, Master," said the genie. It conjured up a bottle of the potion.

Aladdin sneaked into the palace, past Abenazer's guards and found his wife. He gave her the bottle of potion and told her his plan.

Aladdin went to hide and his wife called to Abenazer, "Let me out of this prison and I'll marry you."

Abenazer let Aladdin's wife out and she dropped the potion into his drink. Abenazer started to yawn and soon he was asleep, with the lamp under his arm.

When Aladdin was sure that Abenazer was asleep, he came out of his hiding place. He pulled the lamp from Abenazer's grasp and quickly rubbed it before Abenazer could awake. "Restore my palace and banish Abenazer forever!" cried Aladdin to the genie of the lamp.

In the blink of an eye, Aladdin and his wife were back in their own, splendid palace. The genie sent Abenazer, far, far away, to the other side of the world and Aladdin and his wife lived happily every after.